KU-424-855

HOW MEN
AND WOMEN
WERE MADE

WHY PEOPLE DO
NOT LIVE FOREVER

WHY THE SUN
TRAVELS SLOWLY

Orchard Books
96 Leonard Street, London EC2A 4XD
Orchard Books Australia
14 Mars Road, Lane Cove, NSW 2066
First published in Great Britain in 1998
This edition published in 1999
1 86039 701 8 (hardback)
1 86039 868 5 (paperback)
Text © Margaret Mayo 1998
Illustrations © Tony Ross 1998
The rights of Margaret Mayo to be identified as the author
and Tony Ross to be identified as the illustrator have been
asserted by them in accordance with the
Copyright, Designs and Patents Act, 1988.
A CIP catalogue record for this book is available from the British Library
1 3 5 7 9 10 8 6 4 2 (hardback)
1 3 5 7 9 10 8 6 4 2 (paperback)
Printed in Great Britain

HOW MEN AND WOMEN WERE MADE

WHY PEOPLE DO NOT LIVE FOREVER

WHY THE SUN TRAVELS SLOWLY

RETOLD BY MARGARET MAYO
ILLUSTRATED BY TONY ROSS

 ORCHARD BOOKS

HOW MEN AND WOMEN WERE MADE

At first there was a noisy god of the sky, whose name was Huracan. He was everywhere – in thunder, lightning, wind and rain, darkness and light. But there was also a quieter god, lying on the calm sea, all hidden under shimmering, blue and green feathers. His name was Feathered Snake.

Somehow, sometime, Huracan and Feathered Snake met and they decided to make the earth. Together they said, "Earth! Let it be!"

And the calm sea trembled and bubbled. Big waves rolled across its surface. Land rose up from the depths and rose and rose, until there were high jagged mountains, deep valleys and wide plains.

Then Huracan and Feathered Snake decided to make living things. Together they said, "Life! Let it be!"

And plants sprang up, and the land was filled with colour. The sea was filled with fish. The air was filled with birds and insects. Little creatures scurried through the bushes. The pumas and jaguars bounded up the mountains, and the snakes slithered through the grass.

"Now," said Huracan, when everything was made, "the time has come for the birds and animals to thank us for making them."

"You are right!" said Feathered Snake. Together they said, "Speak! Call our names! Praise us!"

But the birds just twittered, whistled
and squawked, while the animals grunted,
barked, growled and roared. Not one of
them could speak.

"That wasn't good enough!" said Feathered Snake. He was disappointed. "What shall we do next?"

"We shall make a man," said Huracan.

So they took some mud and shaped it and made the first man. He was the same shape as a man is today. But because the mud was soft he couldn't stand properly, he couldn't speak, and when it rained the water washed him away.

"Again!" said Feathered Snake. "Not good enough! What next?"

"We must make a solid man," said Huracan. "One that doesn't collapse."

So they took some wood and carved it and made a wooden man. He could stand and move and talk. The gods were pleased, and they made some more men, and they made some women too. And the wooden men and women had wooden children.

But the wooden people had no thoughts or feelings. They didn't laugh or cry, and their faces were always blank.

The gods were patient. They waited for a while before Huracan said, "The time has now come for the wooden men and women to thank us for making them."

Together the gods said, "Speak! Call our names! Praise us!"

The wooden people heard, but they didn't understand. They didn't know what it meant to be thankful, and they said nothing.

"Yet again!" said Feathered Snake. "Not good enough! What next?"

"I shall destroy them," said Huracan. And he threw down black tarry rain upon the wooden people and drowned most of them. A few of the wooden people, however, managed to escape by running into the forest and climbing trees. They lived on, and their children are still in the trees today. Now they are monkeys – and that is why monkeys look so much like men and women.

Once more the gods met. "I'm not sure," said Feathered Snake, "whether it's possible to make someone who will be  grateful and worship us."

"We must try, once more," answered Huracan. "This time we shall make the man from the seed of the most wonderful plant we have made."

Then they picked some corn cobs. Yellow ones and white ones. They pounded the corn kernels together and added water, and from this mixture they shaped four men.

The men had firm flesh and strong muscles. They stood straight and walked and talked. Besides that, they had feelings. They smiled and frowned, laughed and cried. And they were very clever. When they looked, they could see things that were a long way off. They could even see Huracan and Feathered Snake. They saw everything, and they understood everything. They were like gods.

As soon as they were made, the four men called out, without being asked, "We thank you, Feathered Snake! We thank you, Huracan! You have made us, and we really thank you! Twice! Three times, we thank you!"

But what was this? The gods were not pleased.

"These men are too good!" said Feathered Snake. "They are perfect! They know everything!"

"If they are like gods, they will not look up to us," said Huracan. "They will be our equals, and before long they will stop praising and worshipping." Huracan thought for a while. "I must dim their eyes," he said.

And he blew a mist into the eyes of the
four men, so that they could only see
clearly things that were close, and they
could no longer understand and explain
everything. Then the world seemed full of
marvels and mysteries, and so, again and
again, the men praised their gods,
Feathered Snake and Huracan.

"That's much better!" said Feathered Snake. "Now, have we finished?"

"No," said Huracan. "We must make four women."

They waited until the four men lay down to sleep. Then Huracan and Feathered Snake picked some corn, and made four truly beautiful women, and dimmed their eyes and left them lying asleep beside the four men.

From those four men and four beautiful women came all the people. Their eyes are still dim, and the world, to them, still seems full of marvels and mysteries – and so they praise their gods, again and again.

(A Central American story from Guatemala)   20

WHY PEOPLE DO NOT LIVE FOREVER

In the beginning, nothing ever died. The tortoise and his wife, the man and the woman, the stones, everything there is – lived for ever. It was the Maker who arranged it that way.

But one day the tortoise said to his wife, "I've been thinking. What I'd like most of all is to have lots of little tortoises."

"So would I," said his wife. "That would make me very happy. Let's go and ask the Maker for some."

Off went the tortoise and his wife, crawl, crawl. They came to where the Maker lived, and they said to him, "Please give us some little tortoises."

"Mmmm ... what you want is children," said the Maker. "Think carefully. If you have children, you can't live for ever. A time will come when you must die. Otherwise there will be too many tortoises."

And the tortoise and his wife said,
"First give us children. Then let us die."
"That is how it shall be," said the
Maker.
Then the tortoise and his wife went
home, crawl, crawl. And soon – great joy!
such great joy! There they were – lots of
little tortoise children.

When the man saw all the little tortoise children toddling around, playing with their parents and having fun, he said to the woman, "I too would like to have children."

"So would I," said the woman. "That would make me very happy. Let's go and ask the Maker for some."

Off went the man and woman, big
strides, big strides. They came to where
the Maker lived, and they said to him,
"Please give us some children."

"Are you sure?" said the Maker. "Think
carefully. If you have children, you can't
live for ever. A time will come when you
must die. Otherwise there will be too
many men and women."

And the man and the woman said,
"First give us children. Then let us die."

"That is how it shall be," said the
Maker.

Then the man and the woman went
home, big strides, big strides. And soon –
great joy! such great joy! There they were
– lots of little children.

The stones saw the tortoise children and the human children toddling around, playing with their parents and having fun. But the stones didn't want to have any children so they didn't go to the Maker.

And even now a time always comes when men, women and tortoises must die. The Maker arranged it that way, because they have children. But stones, who have no children, they never die. They live for ever.

(An African story from Nigeria)

WHY THE SUN TRAVELS SLOWLY

When the world was young, the sun used to race across the sky so fast that the days were very short and the nights were very long.

There was never enough daylight for anyone to finish their work properly, and the children – well! they never ever managed to finish their games.

Everybody grumbled. Every day. Grumble, grumble, grumble. But there was nothing they could do to make the days longer.

And then Maui was born. He grew up. He became a man. He was Maui, the hero. The great Maui who knew a thousand tricks.

It happened that early one morning
Maui and his five brothers set out in their
boat to do some fishing. But they had
only just dropped their hooks into the
water, when the sun
plunged straight
down into the sea,
and suddenly it
was dark.

Maui was angry. "We must stop that
sun racing across the sky," he said. "Yes,
you and I, my brothers, must catch her
and make her move slowly so that the
days are longer."

"Maui," said his brothers, "oh, Maui,
no one can catch the sun. No one."

"We shall make a noose," said Maui. "A big strong noose. And we shall catch her."

Truly, Maui knew a thousand tricks, and the next morning he taught his brothers how to twist coconut fibre together and make strong ropes. Then he showed them how to weave the ropes into a big noose with six long ropes attached around the edge – one long rope for each brother.

When night came, and the sun couldn't
see them, Maui and his brothers took the
noose, climbed into their boat and sailed
eastwards. They sailed and sailed until
they came to the pit at the edge of the
ocean where the sun comes up.

The five brothers were afraid, but Maui chanted, "Hold your rope! Hold it firm! And now, together, throw!"

Then they flung the noose over the top of the pit, and each brother held his rope, and together they waited.

Suddenly the sun shot up out of the pit and into the noose and – whoom! the ropes broke. They were not strong enough against the power of the sun.

"Ahhh!" cried the five brothers. "What did we tell you? No one can catch the sun!"

"We shall try again," said Maui.

They sailed home, and the next morning Maui told his brothers to collect all the coconut fibre on the island. So they collected every little bit of fibre they could find.

They twisted it into ropes, and then Maui taught them to plait three strong ropes together to make an exceedingly strong rope. Then, with the plaited ropes, they made another noose.

When night came, Maui and his brothers
took this noose and sailed to the pit at the
eastern edge of the ocean. They set the
noose over the top of the pit. Each brother
held his rope, and together they waited.

Once again the sun suddenly shot up out of the pit and into the noose. The brothers held their ropes tight, and the sun pulled and pulled. The ropes were exceedingly strong but then – sszzzzz! the sun's fierce heat frizzled up the ropes, and she was free.

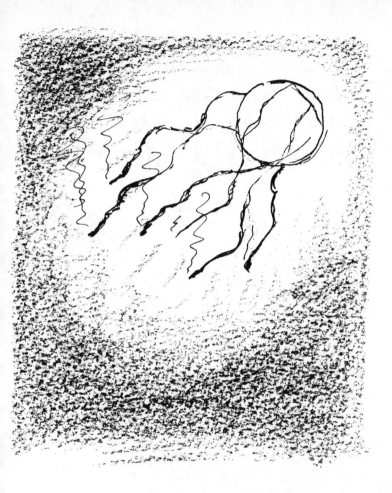

"Ahhh!" cried the five brothers.
"What did we tell you? No one can catch
the sun!"

"We shall try again," said Maui.

They sailed home, and on the way Maui thought of his sister, his one and only sister, the beautiful Hina. He knew exactly what he must do, but it made him sad.

The next morning he
went to see his sister,
who had the most
wonderful long
black hair that
reached right
down her
back.

"Beautiful
Hina," said
Maui, "will
you cut off
your hair and
give it to me?"

"Cut off my
long black
hair!"exclaimed
Hina. "Why
should I
do that?"

"There is power in your hair," answered Maui. "With it, I can catch the sun and make her travel slowly across the sky."

"For this alone, I will cut off my hair," said Hina. And she cut off her wonderful long black hair and gave it to Maui.

Then Maui and his brothers wove a noose with their sister's hair. It was fine and light, and looked very fragile, yet it was wonderfully strong.

When night came, Maui and his brothers took the noose and sailed to the pit at the eastern edge of the ocean, set the noose over the pit and waited.

Once again the sun suddenly shot up
out of the pit and into the noose. The
brothers held their ropes tight, and the
sun pulled and pulled. The brothers held,
held, held and the sun pulled, pulled,
pulled. There was a long struggle, but the
ropes made from Hina's wonderful hair

did not break, and the sun's fierce heat could not burn them. So the sun at last, was caught.

"Let me go!" cried the sun. "Set me free!"

"You must first make a promise," said Maui.

"What sort of promise?" asked the sun.

"You must promise to rise slowly each morning, and to travel slowly, very slowly across the sky, and then to sink slowly into the ocean each night, so that the days are always long enough for everyone to finish their work."

"I give my promise," said the sun.

Then Maui and his brothers let go of their ropes and the sun went on her way slowly, very slowly with the fine noose still wrapped around her and the fine ropes trailing out behind. And the ropes made from Hina's wonderful hair still hang from the sun. Anyone who looks carefully at the sun, when she rises or sinks into the ocean at sunset, can see them stretched out across the shining water.

When Maui, the hero, and his brothers returned home everyone was full of happiness. They could see for themselves that the sun was now travelling slowly, and they were thankful. And, from that time on, the days were longer and the people had enough daylight time to finish their work, and some left over to rest and play. But the children – well! it seems they never ever had quite enough time to finish their games. They always wanted just a little longer!

(A story told in New Zealand and the Polynesian islands)